FOUNTAIN OF YOUTH

Lore-Lovers Erotica ™

Lexus Love

Pussy juice is addictive. Its very essence is life giving...

LADY VON GREY

CONTENTS

Title Page

Copyright

Epigraph

1   1

2   5

3   8

4   12

5   15

6   19

7   22

8   25

9   29

About The Author   31

1

◆ ◆ ◆

1892, in a lone mansion in Kensington Park, London…

Meg laid back onto her right elbow. Her fleshy, bronze-colored thighs were spread wide open as Priscilla continued to dine on her bald pussy lips as she had been doing for most of the day.

"Ahh… yes. You nasty, old, cunt-sucking bitch!" Meg moaned, holding the woman's head in place. She watched as Priscilla's thick tongue continuously slid up and down her hairless folds then enveloped her clit with her thin, pink lips to suck on it like a sugar cube.

Meg's mistress, Madame Bodine would not be happy to know that some white woman, especially one of the prominent society women, was eating her barely 16-years-old, black outcast out alive.

For over four hours now, the woman had had her head buried between Meg's thighs without a break and had somehow kept the girl orgasming continuously on her monstrously long snake-like tongue.

Lady Priscilla had come into the little dress shop on Bond Street and asked the Madam to have a brand new and complete wardrobe made and prepared for a trip across the Atlantic to the new world in one week for an exorbitant price.

She had also paid handsomely to sample the services of the infamous tongue twister that she had orally extracted the information from the chambermaid of her current host.

Caught with her white narrow thighs over her Mistress's houseguest's shoulders the evening of her arrival to England, the young chambermaid had spilled her guts of the infamous pussy muncher that Madam Bodine harbored in the attic of her house.

Having witnessed her mistress being wantonly pleasured so openly by this person in her bed-chamber earlier during the day before her departure to France, the maid would have given anything to keep the old woman's demon tongue stuffed firmly inside her forever.

How unfortunate or fortunate it was for her to orgasm to death, feeding the monster that had inhabited her mistress's home one week later.

With wrinkles visible around her almost none existent mouth, and others lining the paper-thin skin on the back of her hand, Priscilla always needed a quick fix to maintain her youthful looks like Botox.

The English chambermaid was delicious, but she hadn't lasted long, neither had Priscilla's host.

A middle-class socialite with few friends or sponsors, Priscilla had tongued the woman in her private box at the darkened theatre, drinking her victim's life force away even as the lust-crazed women moaned and whimpered her release.

Lady Cornwell watched as her houseguest's thin tongue grow thicker and plunge continuously deep into her womanly folds right there in the box. She had orgasmed intensely when the soloist had hit her peak.

Feeling warm and sexually relaxed, she did not hesitate when her friend has slipped to her knees and shoved her skirts to her waist in the carriage on their way back from the theatre. It didn't stop there.

Lady von Grey had gorged on her swollen flesh on her front stoop while other carriages rode by, in her parlor she got carpet burned from riding the hungry woman's face and magical tongue, and on her roof on the night of her demise in Paris.

Lady von Grey had forced her to climb to the roof of her house in her linen nightgown and forced her to bend over near the chimney.

Her swollen pussy lips were forced open by the raping tongue, hitting the sweet spot inside her clenching depths. She whimpered from the rough violation, but she couldn't help spreading her legs and arching her back even more to allow Lady von Grey her total surrender.

Countless minutes later, Lady von Grey turned her around and lift her onto the warm shelf of the chimney.

"Hold on tight." Lady von Grey whispered against her clit. "You're in for the fuck of your life."

Thin warm lips pulled on the engorged clit, sucking it as a hungry babe does a tit.

"Ahh…Fuck me, Lady von Grey. Eat my pussy." Lady Francesca held on to her lover's head as she worked her clit in and out of the woman's mouth for a long time.

The wet sucking sounds of her flesh drove her to push and pull the older woman's head against her wanton flesh as a wave of intense please and desire washed over her.

Her passionate moans filled the air as she laid back, enjoying her lover's perverted lust for her juicy cunt. Little did she know that these were her last moments alive. Lady Francesca orgasmed her last breathe away into Lady von Grey's mouth.

When the woman did not attend any social events in two days everyone thought that the woman was in France visiting her family and would not be back for quite some time.

Therefore, it was not a surprise to the housekeeper, her husband and her daughter, the chambermaid when the old, formidable woman presented them a letter, supposedly written by the owner of the house, announcing her boarding of this stranger in her house for a few days while she spent more days in France.

Within the first week of her being in the house, Priscilla had deposed of the housekeeper and her husband. This morning she had gorged on the chambermaid as she climaxed one final time, exploding into a cloud of sparkling dust.

Hours later, Lady Priscilla had expressed significant interest in the young black girl after hearing many erotic tales of her extraordinary beauty and talent.

That day in the shop, the young, big-breasted child had been shocked senseless when the wrinkled old woman had forcefully pushed her up against the wall of the back dressing room to ravish her tiny, pink swollen clit and tight virgin hole.

She whimpered and trembled deliciously as the old woman drank and drank of her essence into her weathered body.

With such sweet honey on her tongue and fingers, Lady Priscilla was hooked, discovering that the girl had power in her blood and pussy fluids, which made her a direct descendent of an ancient and powerful voodoo priestess from the Dark Continent.

Lady von Grey didn't waste time as she whispered a few words against the girl's succulent flesh, permanently binding the girl to her for all eternity as she realized that she had finally found for centuries what she had been hunting for.

The binding spell floated around the tight space between the older woman's face and her tasty treat's plump mons, dancing in the air like musical notes, highlighting the lewd act of her lovingly nursing on the girl's pleasure nub.

Within minutes, the girl's sugar walls released its honey and ran freely down onto Lady Priscilla's tongue as she slurped up every drop of cream, the child unknowingly sealing her fate to the hideous creature that was pleasuring her immensely.

2

◆ ◆ ◆

There had been ladies of all circles in the front room being pinned and measured for new day dresses and ball gowns by the other dressmaking attendants, while Lady von Grey's magical tongue stretched and wiggled away inside the foundling's tightness, right up against her tightly shut cervix.

The notes branded themselves onto the girl's dark chocolate skin in bright neon red letters, burning away the course hair completely and painlessly as the woman brought forth a mind-numbing orgasm to the girl, drinking every drop of the deliciousness that squirted out of the girl's pee hole.

Priscilla had cast a spell when her tongue had first brushed up against the girl's innocence in the shop that morning. The thin barrier had shattered like glass and melted away onto her tongue like stretched sugar.

Thoroughly rejuvenated and her thirst quenched for the morning, Priscilla withdrawing her cum-seeking weapon from the worn-out girl's tight folds.

Before she left that day, the woman had demanded that Madam Bodine send only Meg to deliver the clothes and had paid extra for her services and her time.

Meg, who had never experienced such pleasure before, never mentioned to Madam Bodine what had happened in the backroom, deciding to keep the secret for herself to masturbate during the cold, lonely nights.

However, Madam Bodine had seen all and was soaking wet from watching the old high-class woman feeding on the thick lips of the young plump Meg with such abandonment.

With hundreds of pounds in hand, the madam had had all the girls in the shop work night and day, on the clothes, down to the last day before delivery. However, she intended to go back on her bargain for trading Meg's services.

At night, she would fuck Meg's brains out, first feeding the girl her mature snatch, then grind her wet pussy lips against the girl's plump nether lips until they both came.

On the day of delivery, Madame Bodine had cautioned Meg not to leave the hired carriage upon arrival or step one foot into the client's house, or else she would lose a week's wages and would be viciously whipped for her disobedience.

It was too late now. Meg had been in that house for so many hours, that she had lost count of the number of orgasms she'd had.

When the carriage arrived at the house earlier that day, the vehicle weighed down with packages; the woman had shown up in a silk hand-painted robe and had Meg forcefully escorted upstairs into her private boudoir by shadowy footmen where she was swiftly stripped of her one suitable dress.

With their deed done, the shadow men melted in the shadows of the room like silent sentinels.

Strategically placed candles burning brightly, their flickering flames causing the shadows of the room to dance.

Laughing evilly aloud, the older white woman threw off the robe and waved her hand in the air, calling on another unseen force to make Meg's skin freshly washed and clean, making her dark skin glisten with moisture as if she was fresh from a bath.

Meg could not believe it. Her mouth felt minty clean and her body was free of sweat and the pungent smell of day-old wash.

An icy breeze had brushed against her cunny, which had Meg cupping herself for security; only to find out she was now hairless down there.

The initial shock to learn that the naked, white woman before was maybe a witch or the devil's bride was pushed to the back of her mind when the woman walked up to her and pulled Meg's head into her bald, wet, plump folds, something the woman had never done before with any of her past victims.

Frightened for her life, Meg did the only thing she could do well.

Sitting back onto her haunches, Meg opened her mouth and let the woman's dripping wet opening sink onto her skillful tongue.

Throwing her head back, Lady von Grey fed her creamy pussy to her new toy for a change.

In her long life since discovering the overwhelming power of pussy juice and her essential need for such substance to survive, all Priscilla ever did was feed to her heart's content and dispose of the remains of her victims wherever necessary.

From the way young Meg's mouth was sucking on her creamy flesh, Priscilla figured she was trying to offer the old woman as much pleasure as the woman did that first day in the shop and be on her merry way before Madam Bodine even noticed her absence.

3

◆ ◆ ◆

Pleasuring a woman was a well-known pass time for Meg. Many times over the years, since Madame Bodine found her abandoned on the doorstep of her shop ten years ago, she had forced Meg into servicing a select few of the Madame's rich female clients for room and board.

Meg refused to believe that these women were fascinated with her extraordinary feminine beauty and grey eye color.

Nor did she believe her plump arms, rounded stomach, or big-breasted figure contributed to their lust.

Only Madame Bodine knew that the wide flare of Meg's smock was not padding but her feminine assets. Meg was blessed with generously round hips and firm bubble bottom sitting at the base of an impossibly small waist.

Though she wore heavy clothing to hide her curves to prevent men from molesting her in the streets of London, that never stopped the women from molesting her or from feeding her their hairy muffs occasionally.

Her tongue skills were a well-kept secret among the rich and socially fashionable women that frequented the little dress shop that brought Madam Bodine a heavy purse and a luxurious lifestyle, with wonderful living quarters in a fashionable neighborhood on the outskirts of the city.

To ensure that her minor charge never escaped her sight, Madame Bodine even had a special room in the back to have Meg cater to the whims of those special clients.

Having trained the girl herself for many years on the art of how to pleasure a woman with her fingers and tongue in unorthodox ways, Madam Bodine refused all forms of bribery in selling her little tongue slave.

Once, one young debutante demanded that she was to be thoroughly pleasured in the shop's front for her debut that very night.

The girl's aunt had treated her to a new expensive wardrobe and an earth-shattering orgasm from Madam Bodine's resident tongue twister, a first for the teenage girl.

Meg had no choice but to please Madame Bodine's client, whose chaperone had paid handsomely to view the service upfront and center.

The blonde-haired girl's aunt had kept spreading her skinny niece's legs wider, to part the fuzzy wet folds for Meg to lick, even fingering the tight snatch and feeding the juices to Meg, while she sucked on the girl's nipples and tongue.

For close to an hour the girl's aunt allowed Meg to bring the girl close to the edge repeatedly, denying her the pleasure of cumming too soon.

For such cruelty, Meg had had to endure being called cruel names and taunted while tonguing the 15-year-old debutante's blonde hairy snatch.

That had been nothing new for Meg. Most of Madam Bodine's special clients talked that way to help bring themselves over the edge.

"Eat me, you little black slut! I will lock you in my room and ride your face forever, you fat cunt sucker!" the thin girl moaned and trembled, her fingers buried deep into the black girl's long and thick, tightly coiled shoulder-length curls as she watched Meg sucking her pink nub and lap at her insides.

Being allowed to cum by her nipple-sucking chaperone,

she'd held Meg's head in place while she screamed her release away, right there in the front room where Madam Bodine had locked the door and closed the drapes to avoid anyone from interrupting the oral session.

It didn't stop there. The girl's aunt shoved Meg away and dropped to her knees to lick and slurp the pale girl's flesh herself. Having licked and fingered the freshly fucked pussy to another earth-shattering orgasm, the aunt had Meg lick the cream from her fingers and the girl's soaking wet folds as she'd promised the girl that she would drink her juices whenever and wherever she demanded.

That evening the girl had made her aunt keep her promise as she fed the woman her hairless pussy upstairs in her room where she was supposedly dressing for her debut.

Meg had been 12 back then.

Last she heard from eavesdropping onto two gossipers who visited the shop for a fresh dress each, the debutante had married into a wealthy family, demanding her spinster aunt live within her home with her own wing.

The young countess had born her 60-year-old husband, who her father had arranged for her to marry to elevate his family's status, a legitimate heir within their first year of marriage, and had completely abandoned his bed.

Three years later, the girl's aging and impotent husband had discovered why his young supple wife was always closeted away with her aunt when he had barged into her room one night.

Upon discovery, the Duke had caught his wife's aunt's face buried between her quivering pale thighs, hungrily lapping away on her swollen price as the girl held her golden head in place.

The women hadn't even stopped neither did they acknowledge his presence when he barged into his wife's bed-chamber.

The forbidden pleasure she was receiving from her father's youngest sister was too good to give up.

The Duke had recently found out that this was the reason her father had actively sought a marriage between their two families.

The night before the wedding, he had walked in on them lewdly mashing their flesh together and moaning indecently into each other's mouth.

Unbeknownst to the public, the duke now sat nightly, enjoying the interminable nights by watching his lovely young wife being pleasured by her aunt or vice versa. He especially enjoyed watching them pleasure each other to exhaustion.

The older woman had become accustomed to fucking the girl on her back for years, her hand fisted in her golden locks while she moved above the moaning child.

However, that was another story all on its own.

4

◆ ◆ ◆

Meg had never considered that she may not even like the taste of a woman's flesh against her lips or body because she did.

From the tender age of ten, Meg had been conditioning to loving the tangy taste of female flesh on her tongue. Exactly four years after Madam Bodine took her in, she introduced Meg to the sweet taste of pussy.

Madam Bodine had kept her awake that night until she had been deep and thoroughly satisfied.

Biting her lips and moaning loudly into the curtained bed-covers, the madam had instructed Meg on how to pleasure a woman to the brink of madness and over the edge by forcing the ten-year-old to slurp, lick and finger both her holes, hence beginning her secret career as the infamous tongue twister.

However, sometimes, it all became too much for Meg, especially when a few of the clients didn't wash too well or at all and the pungent smell from their privates would cause her to be sick for days after.

This was not so with Lady von Grey.

The Baroness's flesh tasted of strawberries-Meg's favorite- and her juices were like honey on the tongue, which made her suckle the woman's flesh more intimately and with such lust.

During her time being forced to service these pedophile women, Meg had learned many intimate and erotic words to call a woman's flower garden, especially the colorful words they would scream out amid their release.

So here on her knees, Meg pulled the round ass cheeks wide apart and plunged the tip of her tongue into the puckered pink ass hole of the wrinkled, clean-tasting older woman.
Lady von Grey threw her head back and moaned her first anal orgasm in centuries onto the girl's skillful tongue.

Using two of her fingers, she swirled her tongue in and out of the stretched open pink, puckered arsehole for added pleasure. The taste of strawberries strong on her nose, Meg feasted on Priscilla's sweet flesh.

As Meg pleasured Lady von Grey, she had looked into the girl's eyes and introduced herself as her mistress.

Riding her face while standing up for forty minutes, Priscilla continued to stare down at the girl nursing on her swollen flesh.

She admired the girl's beauty as she worked herself to cum twice, her knees buckling as the girl continued to lash her clit with her tongue.

Hunger for the girl's sweet juices consumed her as she'd pulled the girl towards her to tangle her tongue with hers, tasting her own sweet flavor on the girl's tongue.

Scared to death then, Meg had then begged and pleaded on her knees for the woman to let her go home for she didn't want to be whipped.

Not knowing what she was in for, Meg didn't resist when the woman pulled her up to her feet, to push her up against the many pillows propped up against the solid wooden headboard of the king-sized canopied bed, dominating the room.

With her thighs pushed open till her knees were at her side, into the bedcovers, giving the woman a front-row view of her bald and exposed pussy lips, hidden little nub, and pink virgin arsehole.

She rewarded Meg with an uninterrupted view of the woman reaching down to dine on her pussy lips, groaning as she sucked down hard on the chocolate flesh.

Meg stared, abashed and ashamed, her body melting as the woman opened her mouth and slid the longest and thickest tongue that she had ever seen on a human into her folds.

5

◆ ◆ ◆

Meg gasped loudly as the old woman's diving tongue slid deep and slow at first, into her quivering folds. Too turned on to be afraid, Meg cried out when the snakelike tongue grazed her g-spot, causing her juices to flood her vaginal sheath.

The old woman chuckled evilly and hummed into the clenching sheath for more of the ambrosia.

Realizing her tormentor's intent, Meg refused to let Lady von Grey break her.

Within minutes, Meg was biting down hard on her lush lips to keep from crying out as the woman's thin lips were sucking hard onto her pleasure button while her non-human tongue probed deeply into her warm, milking tunnel.

Unable to tear her gaze away from the monster tongue sliding in and out of her tight, fat pussy, she continued to stare down at the woman who intended to fuck her honeyed insides silly with her evil tongue.

Without warning, the end of that snakelike tongue forced

its way past Meg's g-spot and up to her virginal sheath to bump against her virgin cervix.

Being milked by the stranglehold of the girl's clenching walls, ropes of creamy fluid shot out of the undetectable slit at the tip phallus-like tongue through her cervix and into the girl's fertile womb, ruthlessly fucking the girl into an orgasmic seizure, changing the girl from the inside out forever.

The honeyed fluid that had flowed freely down the girl's throat earlier from the woman's hungry folds had begun the change, turning the girl into something non-human.

Alas, when the woman finally detached her mouth from Meg's wet folds and sat back onto her haunches, a young, vibrant face devoid of any lines or wrinkles with the same thin lips and deep forest green eyes, surrounded by little wisps of solid grey hair brushed wet kisses onto her mouth, thanking her for her gift.

A minute later, she attacked the girl's nipples, sucking the virgin tips into her skillful mouth, driving the girl to experience her first nursing orgasm while Priscilla played with her wet folds and tight ass.

It wasn't long before Priscilla was once again stretched out on her stomach licking, biting, and sucking the inexperienced girl's sweet-tasting flesh like a starving beggar at an all-you-can-eat buffet.

Soon after, she had forced Meg to sit on her face while she licked and suckled on the girl's warm flesh. The shaft-like tongue had fucked her tight hole, driving Meg over the edge repeatedly, while the woman had been stretching her virgin arsehole with her fingers, preparing it for its eventual surrender to the cock-like tongue.

When it had worked its way out of her fertile warmth and into her once human bowels, Meg had subconsciously sat up and sunk onto the invading monster in her ass, screaming her release as the beast continued to burrow in and out of her bowels.

The feeling of being ass fucked by an enormous tongue was so intense; Meg had fucked the thing without thought.

Reaching forward, she plunged three fingers into Lady von

Grey's greedy snatch as her own greedy ass gyrated onto the flesh fuck root.

Now, hours later of pleasuring each other senseless, Lady von Grey was dining on Meg's moist flesh once again.

"Oh Fuck! Lady von Grey!" the girl had dropped the von in the last three hours, as she panted and moaned through her series of wet orgasms.

With her hands buried into Priscilla's thick, silver hair, she held the woman's head steady as she fucked her clit in and out of the woman's warm mouth.

The squish, squish, squish wet sound her flesh made caused her to grind her pussy lip against her lover's face.

"What is it in my holes that keep you drinking my juices all day?"

Priscilla thrust her snake-like tongue deep into the girl's honey pot and hummed in her throat, causing the vibrations to travel up into Megan's clenching walls, lapping up all the loosened cream.   She then slipped the pink tongue into the girl's sweet ass, her ass cream delicious beyond words as the orgasm the girl had been riding finally washed through her.

She had taught the girl that three-letter word and loved hearing it on her lips.

Pulling her tongue out of the girl's virgin ass, Priscilla murmured, "You have something that I want, something that I crave. Something that I intend to take from you." Her fingers plunged in the girl's wet flesh with a wet, squishing sound.

Priscilla could not keep her... anything out of the girl's holes. She molested the young, pliable body until the girl was past exhausted, but she never stopped. She would never stop. The girl was just too delicious for her to want to. Now she had changed her human cells for otherworldly ones. The girl could endure the torture, forever.

Pushing the girl's legs further apart, the older woman's arms slid under her thighs reached up to cup both breasts to tease and pluck each nipple, the woman's sinfully skillful tongue thickened and lengthened like an engorged dick and pushed its way back into the girl, slamming against the black girl's cervix.

The girl loved this form of torture, especially in her guts.

"Ahh... Fuck me!" Meg cried out, the pleasure was so severe that she almost blacked out; however, her body just craved more of the intense pleasure.

6

◆ ◆ ◆

There was no pain, just the mounting pleasure of being fucked deeply by a thick, long tongue that strangely felt and acted like a thick cock.

"What are you looking for in there?" she whimpered as Priscilla's tongue wiggled away inside her tight hole.

Priscilla raised her head for a second and whispered, "The fountain of youth, my dear," before plunging her tongue back into her new toy.

You see, Priscilla was a vampiric witch or a Soucouyant, as they called it in French colonies in the west, one who'd lived for over 500 years by sucking on the clits and folds of young, fresh maidens, be them virgins or not.

Her very existence depended on these women's fertile fluids.

She would kidnap them from their local villages, from the deep valleys of the Carpathian Mountains, and feed on them there.

From Central to Eastern Europe, she stalked prey, dragging them back to her lone hut high in the mountains in Romania to suck and fuck them to death, and had repeated the cycle for over the last 500 years.

Too many who lived among the winding valleys of the Carpathian Mountains, Priscilla von Grey was the lone Vampire Witch of the Lore.

They would scare their daughters with tales of her evil deeds and warn many not to get lost in the woods neither day nor night. How close they were to the truth, only her victims knew.

It is said the Brothers Grimm had written the witch in the story of Hansel and Gretel was based on her.

Only the two young children knew the truth of how they came to be in the witch's hut and how they had escaped Priscilla's prison.

Luring them in by the promise of a warm supper to ease their hunger, the children had entered the hut on their own. Having just washed in the stream right outside the hut, they ate until they were full, and stretched out onto the sleeping mat she magically provided for them to nap on.

She had been busy gorging on Gretel's 14-year-old cunt for the third time that day when Hansel distracted her by stabbing her through with a hot poker from the giant hearth in her hut.

The child had somehow awakened from his drugged slumber by his naked sister's loud moaning from being pleasured by the old woman.

Thinking his sister was being hurt or eaten alive, he had grabbed the hot poker and shoved it into the side of the old witch. Priscilla had screamed and dropped the girl.

Revealing her genuine nature to the children, she told them she would kill the boy and feast on his sister's flesh until she died.

Gretel, not too happy that her stupid kid brother had stopped the old woman from licking her insides so good, was not too keen on having him killed and her being eaten alive, literally and painfully.

The girl rushed to her feet and shoved the old woman into the fire of the hearth, grabbed her brother by the hand, and ran out the hut, never looking back.

Priscilla had survived the fire and had to find another victim to feast on, to regain her strength and heal her wounds.

When the children were found lost in the woods, they told an unconventional story of their capture than what had happened, therefore creating a story of the cannibal witch that we know of today.

But Priscilla's story didn't begin with Gretel.

She had discovered the powerful ambrosia like giving force one night when she stumbled upon a young, beautiful but mute woman who had run away from her stepfather's house, from his roaming hands and demanding cock, deep in the woods of the Romanian forest.

7

◆ ◆ ◆

Priscilla had been an old, bent woman who had enjoyed thousands of youthful men for their semen to strengthen her power and youth spells but had lost her beauty and in return, her lust for them long into her prime.

However, one of her more trickster victims had made a deal with another witch that caused a backlash on Priscilla's need for sustenance from men to women. For years, Priscilla fought her urges for young female flesh.

The youthful woman had stumbled upon the witch deep in the forest, late at night, and was cold and in need of some warmth.

Priscilla, the ever-practicing boszorkány, took one look at the young, beautiful, heavily breasted child, and thought of using her for a bloody sacrifice to regain her youthful looks.

However, the girl had fallen into the raging waters of the river to get away from her stepfather. She had been soaked through from her dip in the frigid stream, far beyond her village, which landed her in the witch's territory.

The stream Priscilla had also taken a dip in minutes earlier.

With great difficulty, the girl had expressed her plight to

the old woman, begging for help.

Priscilla had then led the girl to her modest hut on top of the mountain, shrouded by a heavy fog.

On the way up, she had learned the girl was already 16 years old, unmarried, and was still a virgin, old for one so beautiful. Being a mute didn't help in the girl's plight.

She watched the brunette girl undress and try to dry herself before the large hearth and cauldron, for the first time in years felt a fire in her loins.

Priscilla watched the girl swipe the drying sheet to wipe her body down while she still had on her see-through linen smock, giving Priscilla little peaks at her puckered pink nipples, smooth legs, and barely legal pussy.

Her nipples were tight and hardened from the cold. Even eating the warm soup that Priscilla offered her to warm her up and the slurping noises she made, turned the old woman on more than she cared to admit.

The girl had eaten her fill and was stretched out before the fire, contentment making her eyes heavy with sleep.

Within conscious thought, Priscilla had pounced on the lovely girl before her, reaping the see-through shift from her luscious body, her perky breast spilling out of the torn shift.

The girl had screamed, but no sound escaped her lips as she tried to push the old woman off her, but Priscilla was much stronger than she looked.

She'd easily held the girl down as she sucked one of the girl's large nipples into her wet mouth while roughly twisting the other with her fingers.

The girl who kept trying her hardest to throw the old woman off, never saw the slap coming but felt it land hard across her face.

She'd grabbed her stung cheek and stared up with horror as Priscilla shed her own linen shift off with a twist of her wrist.

Priscilla told her that in no uncertain terms was she to move or die as the woman was a witch. The girl laid there, her legs slightly opened, subconsciously tempting the lecherous old woman with glimpses of her tight pink folds.

She could not believe it when the old woman stretched out her little body over hers to suckle her nipples like a newborn babe while fingering the girl's tight, hot insides, her body responding to the tugging of the old woman's thin-lipped mouth.

She was forced to watch the woman palm her large mammary orbs in her long bony hands and suck on her hard tips with such vigor.

She began moaning silently and squirming in the old woman's embrace as the feeling of being suckled caused tiny drops of her feminine juices to coat the fingers trying to break her hymen deep inside her body.

Without meaning to, she suddenly wished she'd allowed her stepfather to suck her nipples more whenever he wanted to use her asshole for his pleasure as often as he'd demanded.

8

◆ ◆ ◆

From age 13, when her breast had become too big to bind her stepfather had had the nasty habit of cornering her in their two-room hut, any time her mother turned her back on him too long.

Pulling the front of her smock down to suck her large nipples into his pungent mouth the day after he married her gullible mother.

She had shoved him away; however, he had cornered her again to molest her nipples into swollen points with his foul-smelling mouth and large tongue.

The night he wed her mother, the perverted bastard had slept with the child nipple in his mouth, sucking on it throughout the night until she shivered from a foreign feeling. His finger then found her hidden nub and rubbed it until she shivered and wet his hand. He sucked the cream from his fingers then attacked her nipples until they were sore.

One night he used her wetness to slick the engorged tip of this shaft and forced his way into her squirming bottom. She cried out in painful silence, but that didn't stop him from molesting her young, vulnerable body while he continued to suckle from nipple to nipple.

At nights, after her mother and baby brother fell into a deep sleep, her stepfather would hold her down and suckle to his heart's content while pounding her tight little ass until she wet her bedding.

Sometimes, even while her mother was in the hut cooking, he would pull her into a dark corner, onto his lap and his fat cock to suckle on her young nipples and fuck her as hard as he could for as long as he could get away with it.

She would whimper and fight him as hard as she could even while he bounced her up and down his swollen flesh, but he knew with her being mute, he could take advantage of her young body without her mother being made aware.

There she discovered the perverted bastard pleasure of having his girthy cock inside her bum while he molested her breasts.

Many times during the day, he would torture her by suckling her nipples, then he would fill her with cock anally as hard as he wanted in the shed, attached to their hut, outback.

He didn't want to get her pregnant, nor did he want to waste his seed, he'd said as he violated her once virgin hole.

Her mother's death a year ago had given him liberty to nurse on her nipples and use her ass openly at their little eating table, in front of her little brother almost every day and night.

If she'd thought about it, she'd have realized how much pleasure she derived from her stepfather's molestation.

Orgasming with him deep inside her non-resisting ass while he sat at the table with her in his lap, his massive cock stretching her asshole while he nursed on her large nipples before or after dinner, brought them both intense pleasure.

Oftentimes he would lay her back onto their small table and pound her slutty depths until they both cried out from the forbidden pleasure.

It was when he demanded he breeds her pussy that she ran away from home.

Now, here she lay being devoured by some old hag, deep in the forest.

The old woman licked her way down the trembling girl's body, to the soft, fleshy folds of her pussy.

When the old woman tasted her first female, light from within and strength like never shot through her wrinkled body, filling her with a hunger for a woman's flesh.

The old woman began slurping on the girl's hard clit like she was slurping on a sticky sugar stick.

Though the girl was disgusted, she could not help shattering like glass when the old woman's tongue slid up and down her tight, wet folds to suckle her hardened button of pleasure, carrying her through multiple ongoing orgasms.

The same little pleasure button between her thighs her stepfather had been hungrily sucking on while he held her down on her furs in her corner of her parent's bedroom when her mother walked into their hut.

She had been trying to push his head away just like she was doing to the old woman now and just like the roughness of him, the old woman seemed to be determined to attach her tongue inside of her pussy. Unknowingly the girl had been rubbing her pussy lips against the old woman's face, her juices flowing freely, causing the old woman to drink her fill.

Her stepfather had laid down the rule that if her mother didn't want to lose her only source of security and food for her children, she would not interfere with his pleasure.

Her mother had sat huddled in a corner while her husband licked her only daughter into an intense orgasm.

Night after night, the girl had been used to satisfy the old man's lust.

Months later her mother had died from a terrible cough. After the burial in the village's burial plot, her stepfather had wasted no time drilling her ass hard and fast when they got to the hut.

Throwing her down onto his sleeping furs, he licked and fuck her ass hard. She had begged him to stop by trying to fight him but his tongue and fingers invaded her private parts, forcing her to orgasm and lay meekly under him as he filled her ass to the brim with cock.

For hours, she had endured his lust, as he fucked her in many positions with his rock-hard shaft well into the night.

The next morning, he had told her he would wed her by the next eve and breed her to give him more sons. That had been the last straw. As much as she knew being mute would not get her any suitors or married, the girl had run away that same night.

Now, her cumming in this wrinkled old woman's mouth was just as bad as cumming on her stepfather's cock when he sodomized her tight sphincter.

With surprising strength, the old woman curled the girl's body for better access as she sat back on her haunches. The old woman lapped and slurped on the girl's clit like a small dick and tongued the girl's wet holes.

By then the girl's hands were in the woman's loosened snow-white bun, which had magically grown longer and fuller by the second, grinding the old woman's face into her wet cunt.

Her body shook violently as another orgasm rocked through her body to her soul. By the eighth hard orgasm, the girl was riding the old woman's face until she passed out.

9

◆ ◆ ◆

By the time she regained consciousness, a young voluptuous woman's lips were glued to her pussy, forcing her to come repeatedly with her thick and long tongue. The witch had kept the girl alive, imprisoned for one week in that hut.

The girl hadn't known in that in one week her body would no longer bear the supple nectar to give the old witch her strength and youth she required. She didn't know that soon she would be reduced to a pile of sparkly ash, causing the witch to repeat the ritual of hunting, kidnapping, and sucking the very youthful essence out of thousands of maidens.

Hundred of years later, Meg was now bound and caught in the sensual web of the oral desire, which drove her over the edge continuously for hours. Her lustful cries of forbidden pleasure ran out high and far throughout the darkened house as she was forced to feed the insatiable witch that her bound herself to the girl for eternituy , her days were numbered as the bountiful fountain of delicious pussy juice to her new madam.

◆ ◆ ◆

One week later, Ms. Priscilla von Grey, a rich rancher's mail-order bride, was seen boarding a ship with a young black girl with extraordinary grey eyes in tow.

Throughout the long three months voyage, the two barely ate or left their cabin. Even during the storms raging along the Atlantic Ocean, the erotic sounds and screams coming from their room were never heard by any of the passengers or crew members of the ship as it made its way from London to the New World.

Night and day, they remained locked in their room , living off each other's pussy juices. No one was sure if the two were alive or dead.

With a spell cast on the room, no one saw how many times the young, plump, black maid of Lady von Gray named Meg continuously fed her mistress her creamy pussy juice from every inch of their small room nor how often the silver-headed older woman mounted her cunt slave, tribbing their hot pussy together until they were too tired to move from cumming so much.

Mashing their pussies together, Priscilla discovered new ways in making her lover moan and cum over and over again, until the girl was to exhausted to cum.

Three months later, at dawn, the ship docked in the city of New York, where Madame von Grey and her black maidservant checked into their booked room at the newly built hotel and spent the night without taking any refreshments from the hotel's dining hall.

Two days, with three of the female upstairs maids suddenly missing from the town, Madam von Grey and her servant girl moved to upstate New York, never to be seen again.

ABOUT THE AUTHOR

Lexus Love

Lexus Love is a wife and has an established career in customer service. Hailing from the beautiful island of St. Lucia, the Helen of the West Indies, her hobbies are writing, reading, and watching African movies. She lives at home with her husband and their fur baby, Chonkers.

www.ingramcontent.com/pod-product-compliance
Lightning Source LLC
Chambersburg PA
CBHW020853160726
47993CB00004B/1631